FOR HER LOVE

DAKIARA

First Printing: 2019

ISBN 978-1-951271-04-6 Paperback

ISBN 978-1-951271-05-3 Ebook

Additional copies of this book and others are available by mail or by visiting the website listed below. Check website for pricing.

Mind Flow Publishing & Production LLC

PO Box 48768 Cumberland, North Carolina 28331-8768

www.mindflowpublishingproduction.com

Cover design by Carrie & Co.

Editing by Stories Matter Editing

Formatting Design by Under Cover Designs

Dedicated To My Loves
DAQUAN, DEJA, DANTE,
KEVONN AND KIARA

RIP
DAQUAN JAMIQUE 95
&
KIARA DENISE 00

Special Thanks
To GOD for Giving Me
The Strength and The Words
To Do This Project.
Blessed by The Experiences to Draw From
It Has Not Always Been Easy.

Dedicated to Some Who Have Gone Before Me
Mary Merriman
Naomi Thompson

PROLOGUE

"Yo Aiya, it's time to go. Are you coming or not?"

Aiya almost despised the fact that she had invited Sienna to come to the club with her. Sienna didn't miss an opportunity to throw things in Aiya's face.

"You knew he wasn't any good. Come on let's go."

The scene that they had just witnessed wasn't the man she had grown to care deeply for. She admitted that even though they weren't together anymore she still cared about what happened to him. She often tried to talk to him about getting high and acting irresponsibly but when it came to him and his boys, she seemed to always come in second. But what do you expect? All the women wanted him, and all the dudes wanted to be him. He was the small-town boy who made it big. He was living the life that most only dreamed about. No matter how mad she wanted to be, when he smiled that always melted her insides.

Aiya Jones came from a typical middle-class family. The youngest of three children she was often referred to as the mistake of the group. They would say this jokingly, but she was determined not to be a mistake. Her parents were a little older when she came along. They weren't expecting her, but she wasn't going to be denied. Frances went into labor when she was seven months pregnant. Aiya came out kicking and screaming. Her legs and arms were just flailing about.

The doctor said, "She is going to have a set of lungs on her, perhaps she'll be the next Mariah Carey."

As soon as Aiya was placed on Frances' chest, she calmed down.

"This one is special," the doctor said. "You can expect great things."

From a young age she knew she wanted to be an artist. Her parents had taken her to an art gallery when she was eight, and she fell head over heels in love with the different ways that people found to express themselves. From that moment on she always had paper out doodling and creating. Her gift showed itself at an early age and her hunger never let up.

By the time she was in high school, Aiya was entering national drawing competitions and ranking with the best of them. None of those accolades seemed to phase her too much, she simply loved creating, to allow her emotions to have a visual representation. With each year of experience came more under-standing of dimensions and color gradients. To her amazement there were a few gallery owners who wanted to commission her to do some art for them.

While attending Gerrod's School for the Arts, she began working towards her dream of one day owning her own art gallery. In her gallery she would showcase the new and up and coming artists. She wanted to give people the same opportunity that she had to get their work out there in the public eye. Until she saved enough for the space and had enough artwork to even begin her gallery, she worked as a waitress at one of the local night clubs.

Aiya thought she had her life all figured out. Throughout school she had remained focused on her goals. Until one fateful night, in comes Ahmad Sanders or AJ as he was often called.

Ahmad often went by his stage name and loved living the life of his bad boy persona. Ahmad was a fine piece of man candy. His skin was a soft caramel hue. He sported a head full of gorgeous locs.

They even smelled nice, which was a plus. His smile showed off a mouth full of almost perfect teeth. He had a small gap and he had a chipped tooth. None of that took away from the fact that when he smiled, he lit the entire room up. People were attracted to him like the moth is inevitably drawn to the flame. Ladies wanted him, and all guys wanted to be him.

Ahmad was from a single-parent home where his father Tyris often worked long hours at Smitty's Glass Factory. When he wasn't working, he spent a lot of his time hanging with the wrong type of crowd. Tyris used to be a singer back when he was younger. He and his cousins had a group called Harmony3. Ahmad grew up watching his father singing and living the life in the fast lane. With that came the drug use, and the drinking, and the women that inevitably followed. His father would often end up fighting with someone at his gigs. It was during one of those fights, he was stabbed in the throat. Unfortunately, there was severe damage to his vocal cords and his voice would never be the same. Harmony3 began to slip in the bookings having to take any gig their manager could get them booked for. After each fight at the club he would come home and take his frustrations out on Ahmad and his mom, before she finally had enough and packed her bags and left. Angelic gave no reason, she just packed and left. She walked away from Ahmad as if he wasn't her own blood, leaving him at the mercy of an absentee parent.

Ahmad wanted to hate her for leaving him to deal with it, but he understood, she just couldn't take it anymore. He often thought she might come back for him. But that never happened. By the age of 15, he was off getting high with his friends. At the age of 17, right before graduation he got into some trouble by breaking into a drug store with some friends. His friends ran off and left him to take the rap for it. He stayed in jail through the weekend and that scared him almost straight. Ahmad decided that wasn't the life for him.

Ahmad and his friends Slim, and Boogie decided they would revamp his dad's group Harmony3. They renamed the group The Voices of Harmony3. Tyris was happy that his son had decided to follow in his footsteps, so he did all he could to keep him focused. After his run in with the law, Tyris didn't want to see his son go down the wrong road.

"If you are going to pursue this music thing, you have to be serious and dedicated son."

Before he knew it Ahmad, Slim and Boogie were performing in local talent shows and making some serious noise. For a graduation present, Tyris convinced a few of his old contacts in the industry to come to a show and see the boys perform. One of the guys was from Mind Flow Records. Which was the same label that handled his father's career. Of the reps who came to check them out, a guy named Joey B, showed the most interest.

That was the moment Ahmad and his crew were signed to a major record label at the age of 18. With the deal came some contractual obligations from Joey B, he had seen too many young groups fall on their faces with nothing else to fall back on. Talent can only get you so far in life he would always tell them. For this deal to be legit, they all had to enroll in college courses. It wasn't that he didn't believe in them, but he wanted them to be prepared for life no matter what. He hoped they would major in business, so they would be able to handle themselves in the future.

Aiya was the average girl next door except she had goals. She wasn't about to let anything deter her from reaching those goals. Working at the club, she had access to The Voices of Harmony3, that was one of the perks. The club had signed them as one of the house performers. When they weren't touring and making others swoon, they were entertaining the hometown crowd. Aiya liked the fact that to the guys in the band she was invisible. There was no pressure, she could listen to their music and relax.

One Friday night, when Aiya arrived at the club for her shift, the owner Maxx seemed a little troubled. This was the first time she had seen his frown lines that deep in the last four years that she worked there. In that moment, he looked every bit of his sixty-five years. Most days he barely looked forty-five.

"Maxx, what's wrong? Why are you looking so upset?"

Maxx was so into his own thoughts he didn't notice Aiya as she stood mere inches away from him.

"It's nothing kid, at least nothing for you to worry about."

"I know when something is wrong Uncle Maxx, yes I just played the family card."

"I have to find another group to play here at the club."

Aiya, immediately looked around, and saw the stage no longer had the banner she had grown accustomed to seeing. The one that announced to all the patrons that the Voices of Harmony3 would be performing that night. With a deep sigh, Aiya asked what happened. Maxx shook his head and stated, "Another great voice wasted."

Handing her the crumpled-up article in the newspaper. The article read, Local Artist at Fault in a Two-Car-Collision. Drugs and Alcohol Involved, was the subtitle. Aiya could only shake her head. That was the last she heard about Ahmad.

ONE

SEVERAL MONTHS LATER

"It is good to be going home. I know I can be different. I will be better than ever".

Will didn't comment at all; he had heard this line many times. In fact, each time Ahmad was arrested, or sent to the quick fix rehabs, which never seemed to work very long.

Will had been Ahmad's agent since he signed his contract five years ago, although most days he felt like he was herding cats, the guys constantly had him on the move putting out one PR fire after another. Joey B had entrusted Ahmad's success or his downfall to Will. In this case it didn't help that Joey B was also Will's father, so he felt pressured to ensure his first ever client was a success.

"Good to see you man. How are you feeling? You look refreshed and clean."

Ahmad flashed his million-dollar smile.

"Man, I am ready to work. I'm never going back. Yeah, yeah, I know, you've heard me say that before, but man this time I promise."

"I'm glad you feel that way. We need to talk, but let's get you through the doors first. Just a warning, there are quite a few cameras. They will be rolling so watch what you say." Ahmad smirked, "You know me man, only positive vibes."

Will shook his head, that was the problem, he knew him all too well. As soon as they walked through the outside doors, flashbulbs erupted. Ahmad was relieved to be finally going home, but he was agitated by the number of reporters and paparazzi pointing cameras in his face. One shoved a camera too close for comfort, but Ahmad resisted snatching the camera and breaking it. That was something he had done far too often in the past. Then there was the one time, he tried to strangle someone with their camera strap. Will was nervous about his client's release from The Haven, an exclusive drug and alcohol rehab facility that catered to the rich and famous. He leaked Ahmad's release date and time to try and test him. So far, he was pleased at his response. Maybe he was actually ready for part two of Will's plan that was guaranteed to get his meal ticket back on top. A sudden flash interrupted his thought.

"Do you think Ahmad is ready to be discharged? Has he truly changed? You can say what you want, we know he will be right back here real soon."

Will was immensely annoyed. Looking over at Ahmad though calmed him down. He was smiling and working the crowd all the way until he got into the awaiting car. After a few moments of silence, Will let him in on part two of the plan.

"Listen Ahmad, today I tested you. I called the paparazzi and the reporters and leaked when you would be discharged."

Ahmad's smile turned into a look of displeasure.

"Wait, wait before you go getting upset. I had to make sure that you learned your lesson and you were ready for a change."

"What do you mean a change? I'm clean, for the first time in years. That is a change for me. I told you I'm not going back."

"That's just it," Will interjected.

"I want to make sure you don't. We need to show the world a toned down, mature, less aggressive side of you. You know a softer side. What do you think?" Ahmad looked astonished; he couldn't believe he was hearing all of this.

"Will, are you suggesting that I'm some out of control boorish oaf?"

"No, not that, but you have been notoriously out of control in the past. Everyone you've been with as far as relationships, last less than two weeks."

"What can I say? I love them and leave them. That way I don't get hurt."

Holding his head, and shaking it,

"You don't get it. That makes you a callous playboy, who gets high and runs all over people like they're not even there. Is that the legacy you want to leave behind? Just listen to my plan, it will work,"

"I'm good as is man, if you don't believe in me, that is on you. I will prove you wrong."

"You just don't get it. I'm trying to help you. Just hear me out here."

Neither man noticed that they were getting closer to their destination. Will didn't think Ahmad would honestly put up this much of a fight.

"Ahmad, I have arranged for you to meet a young lady. The two of you will become an item. It will be for publicity only but for the world it will be real. I think she can handle you and help you at the same time. Yes, I know you don't think you need this, but trust me my friend you do. You really do. Your album sales have plummeted, and they are so far in the toilet the only way to resurrect them is by doing something drastic like this. Before you say it, yes, I have already spoken with your dad and he is all for it. Even he has seen this work in the past. I just need to know that you are onboard with it and willing to play along."

"No, I'm not."

Taking a deep breath, Will leaned in close and whispered, "I hate to be this way, but if you want to maintain your deal with

Mind Flow Records, you're going to do this and make it look legit."

Will had never had to threaten him to do anything before. He felt amateurish for having to stoop to that level and act that way, but he had to secure the deal. Ahmad sat back in his seat, his eyes glaring and piercing right through Will. He couldn't believe he used his contract to force him into this sham of a relationship.

"You got me. It's either this or I'm out correct?"

Will felt horrible. He knew it was for his own good.

"Just agree to meet her and we will go from there." Ahmad reluctantly agreed.

TWO

AIYA

Aiya's phone had been ringing nonstop while she was working on a piece.

Normally she would put on the do not disturb feature, so it doesn't break her concentration. She pauses her work on the piece to take a break for a snack. During the break she takes the opportunity to check her notifications. Will, her cousin had called numerous times. Hitting the button to redial the number, her cousin answers on the first ring.

"Will, whats going on? I haven't heard from you in a while. Is everything okay?"

"Hey Aiya, yes things are just fine, I have a proposition for you. You know you're my favorite cousin, right?"

Listening intently, Aiya takes in what Will is asking of her.

"So, let me get this straight. You want me to do what? Participate in a fake relationship?"

It wasn't the most outlandish thing she had ever heard, but still she had a lot on her plate right now. Her grandmother's health was failing, and the family decided hospice was the best course of action. Aiya's parents were getting up there in age themselves, trying to provide care for her granny was draining them physically as well as financially, as well as Aiya. Her siblings weren't much help in this aspect. Chase, Aiya's oldest sibling would rather hang out in the strip clubs instead of being there for their parents. Not surprising though, his wife of two years was pregnant and expecting their first child. Chase didn't want a baby yet, she was ready, he chose to act as if his family wasn't growing before his eyes. Sienna was the middle child. She was busy away at Law School trying to change the world. She was drowning in student loan debt so she couldn't help out with much either. Breaking into her thoughts, Will offered to compensate her for her time.

"Will, you could hire anyone to do this for you. Why are you bothering me with it?"

To which Will hesitantly replies, "I know you can handle what I'm asking and besides you will be getting paid. Way more than you make at the club. I know you are trying to get your own gallery. And helping your mom and dad with all the medical bills, can't be easy. All you have to do is meet my client tonight for dinner, just to get a feel for each other. Come on baby cousin, do me this favor, please with a cherry on the top." Finally, she agreed to meet at Barcelona for dinner at 7:30pm.

Barcelona was an amazing Italian restaurant that had just opened. The waitlist was enormous to get a reservation. Aiya wondered how long he had been planning this, because no one jumps that list. They were a stickler for the rules. She was equal parts excited and reluctant about dinner that night. What would she wear, and how would she do her hair were the main questions on her mind. Briefly, the thought occurred "what if he doesn't like me?", she laughed that off. Of course, he would like her, she was amazing and if he didn't think so, then that was his loss. Aiya's hair was past her shoulders and still had its natural curl to it. For tonight's date she decided to wear it down and loose.

Aiya arrived at Barcelona at exactly 7:30. She was promptly

shown to her table and dinner companion for the evening. A smile crept across her face when she realized it was Ahmad. She was pleased when he smiled back. Oh God, his smile was perfect. So many times, she had stolen glances when they were at the club. She was never this up close and personal though. Proximity changed things. When she walked over with the maître d, Ahmad stood up and pulled her chair out for her. Aiya checked that off the imaginary checklist she had running in her head. His attire this evening matched hers to a t. she had settled on a royal blue strapless cocktail dress. Ahmad stood before her, with a black suit, royal blue shirt, with blue and black loafers.

Stammering for his words, Ahmad struggled to get his bearings about him, it was like all his charm and charisma that he relied on to get into a woman's good graces went flying right out the window.

"Good evening, I'm Ahmad. Thank you so much for joining me for dinner tonight."

She couldn't believe he didn't at least think she was familiar from the years the spent working at the same club. Then again, she could, she was invisible to his type. Aiya smiled and introduced herself. It took every ounce of her willpower to not throw in the fact that they used to work in the same club for a few years. That information she decided she would keep to herself. After all this was supposed to be a positive thing.

Within a few minutes the waiter came and saved them from the awkward silence. He suggested a wine to start. Ahmad shook his head and stated he only wanted water with lemon. Aiya requested the same, she knew he was just out of rehab. She didn't want to tempt him. She would never live it down if she was the cause of him suffering a setback causing him to return to rehab so soon after his release. When the waiter returned with their drinks, Aiya asked for some calamari as an appetizer.

"You do know what that is don't you?" Aiya stated matter of

factly, "I do and if you behave you can have some of my squid."
Ahmad looked impressed that she knew what that was.

"Most people tend to get it confused with octopus, but me
being a seafood lover, I know the difference very well."

She couldn't resist that parting jab. How dare he think I am
not knowledgeable? She thought as she placed her napkin in
her lap.

Moments later the calamari arrived, the waiter set out two
saucers for them to share the appetizer. Aiya urged Ahmad to get
some. He dug in. Aiya decided to change the direction of the
conversation a little.

"You are looking quite handsome tonight. I didn't get a
chance to tell you earlier. Those colors compliment you well."
Ahmad blushed and returned the compliment.

"I hope I wasn't staring too much. You look amazing. The
color you chose really brings out your eyes. The blue sets your
skin tone ablaze. Exquisitely matched."

That simple conversation indeed changed the outcome of the
evening. Both became more relaxed with each other and the
conversation began to flow easily between them. Each telling the
other snippets of their lives. When Aiya finally disclosed that
they frequented the same club for the last few years, Ahmad's
mouth dropped.

"I knew I had seen you before, but I just couldn't place
where. You know I've had a rough go of it for the last few
months."

He smiled, "But that's all behind me now though. I'm clean,
I'm sober, trying to live my best life." Aiya shook her head in
agreement.

"That is great to hear. You deserve to be happy. When will
you return to the music industry? Will you and the guys still
continue with the group?"

This one was inquisitive that was for sure. She without effort
had made all of his past conquests pale in comparison.

The rest of the dinner progressed well. They began to laugh and giggle a bit. They talked about the awkwardness of the first few minutes. Aiya was more surprised than anything. From seeing him at the club, she didn't give him much credit. Ahmad was a womanizer without a doubt, at least that was how she saw it. The women would swoon around him, constantly throwing themselves at him. He could have made it harder, but she knew he and the other guys enjoyed it. She had to give him credit though, he could sing the panties off a lady, before they made it to the chorus.

Even from the bar, she had fallen under his spell a few times. Tonight, at dinner she began to see him in a different light. Over dinner they both learned they shared a love for art, as well as they were history buffs. They were both obsessed with learning about their ancestry as well as exploring other cultures. It was funny and comforting they both wanted to travel to Japan. That was on their bucket list of things to do. Perhaps they would do it together. The pair both entertained the same thought and smiled unaware that they were thinking the same thing.

Aiya was glad she made the trip to Willows Peak, for this meeting. When the two parted company, Ahmad insisted on walking her out to her car. He leaned in and kissed her on the cheek and whispered goodnight in her ear. This was a normal move he made on women, most fell for it and would turn in and kiss him on the lips. That would be when he knew he was not going home alone that night. Aiya made no move to turn in. This act alone piqued his curiosity even more than the whole dinner. She wasn't easy, she knew her worth and was going to make whoever she was with earn her respect and affection. Now so did he.

THREE

AHMAD

Ahmad was awakened from his slumber to the strident sound of his phone ringing. He reached over and checked the caller id. With a long pause, he sighed and answers.

"Hey man, how was last night? I called you several times and you didn't answer. Was everything okay?"

"Dude, how can I answer the phone if I'm eating dinner with a lovely companion. What is so urgent that you couldn't wait for a decent time to call. Its only 10 am."

Will wasn't sure how he would take the next part of the conversation.

"I'm outside your door. Can you open it please?"

Ahmad eased off the bed, throwing on his favorite plush robe, with his name embroidered on the back. Without hesitation, Will dove right in as soon as the door opened.

"It's time to go home my friend. Back to where it all began, Geronimo Falls."

Ahmad didn't know if he was ready for that. He hadn't seen or spoken with his father since he was released from rehab. Ahmad knew his father was disappointed, but how could he judge? His own life was jacked up because he chose the same path as his only son.

"I know you have reservations of seeing your father, but this is crucial to the course we chose to get you back on track and back into the good graces of the public. They will worship you again. Small town kid, makes it big, falls short, but then redeems himself. Your fans will eat it up Ahmad."

There was no more fight in Ahmad, and he agreed to go home. He wasn't just going home though. He was about to meet Aiya's parents.

"Whoa, you want me to what? This was supposed to be just a fake relationship. You want me to meet her parents. That sounds pretty official to me Will. I mean call me old fashioned, but I don't know her well enough for that yet. Yeah, we had a cool time last night, but that was an awkward coerced date. Yeah it ended well but still that was only a few hours. Maybe after a few dates, I will be ready for that."

"What would make you more comfortable Ahmad, because this is going to happen. You having to face your dad, and meeting her family is a requirement. You remember what we talked about right? If the public gets an inkling that this relationship is a set-up, they will try you in the court of public opinion. And there is no escaping their judgment once it's been handed down."

As much as he hated to admit it, Will was right.

"I will go on one condition."

Will who had turned and faced away from Ahmad, turned back to face him.

"Name your condition."

Feeling full of himself, with a sly grin he coolly stated he wanted another date with Aiya. This time he wanted to meet her at a beach that was nearby. To this Will agreed with an additional request of his own.

"You will have to call her and invite her yourself. That way you can agree on the time and exact place."

The two men shook hands. Will turned to leave, but hesitated and calmly said to Ahmad,

"Be careful with my cousin. She isn't like your other groupies. Arrangement or not, she is family. I only brought her in because she is perfect for this, and she is in a bind financially. Aiya has too much going for her to throw it all away. She is flawless in my book. So be careful my friend."

Putting his hand to his chin, rubbing his rugged but well-kept beard, Ahmad replied,

"No worries bro. She is extraordinary so far. Nothing like the others."

Smiling to himself as he walked towards the door, "So, make the call, you're burning daylight."

After showering and getting something to eat Ahmad decided that it was time to call her. He had gotten the number from Will before he left. For the first time in his life he was nervous when it came to a female. Trying to shake it off and regroup, he looked into the mirror and repeated out loud, "Man you got this. You aren't no punk. Just call her already." The pep talk didn't help very much. He played with the phone for a few minutes. Ahmad dialed the number and hung up as soon as he heard the first ring. He played this torturous game for a while. When he began his 10th time calling, before he could press the button, his phone was ringing. Smiling to himself and shaking his head, he wiped his hands on his jeans and answered. Prepared to tell a white lie about all the hang up calls, he was caught off guard when she spoke. Her voice was intoxicating even through the phone. Aiya's simple "Hello", was almost more than he could stand.

"Hello, was someone trying to reach me?"

Clearing his throat, he finally managed to squeak out, "Ummmm yes, it's AJ, I mean Ahmad. I was trying to call and

let you know how much of a good time I had last night but my
phone kept freezing up. My apologies. Hey, since I have you on
the line, I have a question for you. I wanted to know if you
would like to go to the beach with me tomorrow. I was trying for
today, but I only just recently got your number from Will."

Aiya smiled and he could feel it through the phone. Her
smile was electrifying, her teeth were gorgeous. That made
Ahmad self-conscious about his own smile for the first time
since he was a kid. He had gotten into a fight with two guys over
Claudie, one of his ex's. Ahmad always had a small gap, and
now he had a chipped tooth. He thought about repairing it but
felt like it added to his bad boy persona.

Aiya interrupted his thoughts, "I can meet you today if you
like. My schedule is pretty clear, for the foreseeable future."

She let out a wry chuckle. The thought that she put her life
on hold for him gave him pleasure but also burdened him. What
if it didn't work out pretend or not? Then again, she was getting
paid, so it wasn't a total loss. It is just a business deal man. Stay
focused, he told himself. Play this calm, cool, and collected. He
remembered his father's words about dealing with women; never
let them see you sweat.

"So, Ahmad where would you like to meet up at? Which pier
do you prefer 1 or 3?"

"How does pier 1 at 1 sound? Make sure you dress comfort-
ably and that includes the shoes. I'd like to walk and talk if you
are good with that."

Aiya agreed and hung up the phone. There was something
about this man, there always had been.

Time rushed by, before Ahmad knew it, he was standing on
the beach, with only a blue tank top, khaki shorts and his favorite
Nautica flip flops on. In his hand was one single white rose. He
didn't want to be corny and show up with a dozen roses, because
where would she put them as they walked. He remembered how

gorgeous her hair was and thought this one would tuck perfectly behind her ear without too much trouble. When he saw her, she was coming up on his left side, as he turned, she could see the rose in his right hand. She simply smiled. It's amazing how something so simple can mean so much.

They greeted each other with a quick hug, he kissed her cheek right on her dimple. This made her smile. She thought to herself, he paid attention or maybe it was just a stroke of luck. Ahmad knew in that moment that he enjoyed seeing her smile. Aiya loved his smell. If she wasn't mistaken it was the cologne Eternity. She had caught a few whiffs of it at the club and always associated it with him.

Ahmad presented her with the rose. She gestured for him to place it behind her ear. He willingly complied. It looked good on her. At that moment he extended his hand for her to grab, she did, and they entwined their fingers. They began their walk hand in hand. When their hands first connected, they both jumped a little, almost as if they were shocked by a static force. Both smiled.

They began their walk, strolling casually up the strip of the beach. The two of them let the water run between their toes. After a while, Ahmad struck up the conversation as to why she was doing this. She said she remembered always seeing him at the club, he looked lost even though he was with his boys and his fans.

"You were enjoying your life but ruining it at the same time. I thought you were someone who deserved a second, well probably more like tenth chance at happiness. I know singing makes you happy. Truth be told, it isn't all about you and your comeback. I'm getting paid to pretend to be into the hottest guy around. The money I'm getting will help with some medical bills for my grandmother and help me get one step closer to opening my gallery. Then, I too will be happy. It's a win-win for both of us."

The conversation between them felt natural and not forced. Surprisingly they held onto each other's hand the entire day only letting go to sit down and eat. As they were getting up to leave, a couple passes by, but suddenly doubles back. The guy starts saying despicable things about Ahmad.

"Well, if it isn't the singing junkie. Lady if you know whats good for you, you will stay far away from him... he is no good. I don't know you, but I do know that you deserve better."

The female was just standing there laughing while her guy continued harassing them. To Ahmad's surprise Aiya, walked closer to the couple.

"Why don't you two go somewhere else and mind your own business. We are simply trying to enjoy ourselves, not be harassed."

The female chimed in, "You going to let your girl do your talking? You are so lame, and to think I used to have a crush on you. Dodged a bullet there."

Without hesitation Aiya reached out and slapped the chick with her left hand, all without letting go of Ahmad's with her right. Ahmad instinctively tried to pull her back, but she stood firm and when the guy started up again, she popped him also. Ahmad didn't know what to do, whether to smile as he was already or pull her away from danger. He decided to follow her lead.

"If you guys have anything else to say, you can take it up with me, his girlfriend. I'm not sure why you thought you could just come around and spew your vitriol around like it is harmless. Yeah, he might have screwed up, but he is working on being a better human being. Which is more than I can say about the two of you."

Unable to stand anymore of this spectacle, Ahmad coaxed his girlfriend away. Did he just use that term even in his head?

"Aiya listen, I really appreciate you taking up for me. That was surprising to say the least and I'm touched that you would do that for me. By the way, my girlfriend huh? So, we are really going to go through with this?"

She shook her head affirmatively.

"Let me see your hand to make sure you are okay."

"I'm okay, are you okay? How could you not react when they said those things? That goes to show you are a better man than you used to be. I recall at least three fights you were in at the club. I believe that is where that lovely chipped tooth came from."

Ahmad turned away from her, that chipped tooth was like a glaring reminder of his previous lifestyle, not to mention it made him aware of his flaw. Aiya gently placed her hand on his and guided his face back towards her. Without thinking she kissed him. It wasn't the peck on the cheek they previously shared. They both seemed to feel it, instead of breaking away from one another, they clung to each other as if their lives depended on it. Finally, Aiya pulled away breathlessly, her lips swollen from their shared passion. Ahmad didn't let her go that easily. He now caressed her face with both hands cupping it and pulled her in for yet another tantalizing kiss.

"It's getting late, I need to get home soon, it is a short drive but a lonely one. This sun has been beating down on me out here. Don't get me wrong, I will admit that I am enjoying myself more than I thought I would."

Ahmad shook his head in agreement. Which each shake, his locs also agreed. Aiya had never seen locs on a male so well maintained and sweet smelling. His locs dangled just below his firm butt and smelled of a mixture of mango and papaya. Aiya thought, not too long and not too short. When they reached the parking lot, Ahmad opened the door after she unlocked it. Turning to get into her blue Honda Accord Aiya's body brushed up against his. Each time they touched whether accidentally or encouraged, she could feel the electricity arcing between them like it was a tangible force. She knew he had to feel it too. She was a bundle of nerves while he remained calm, cool, and sexy. There was no denying he was the whole package. Any woman would envy her if she was with him. Aiya wasn't too shabby herself. She was not only gorgeous, talented and she could handle herself if the need arose. The two of them were a dangerous combination.

FOUR

AIYA

Several weeks had gone by, Aiya and Ahmad had spoken on the phone or hung out almost every day.

Surprisingly enough they were both starting to open up to each other. It almost didn't seem like they were following a script. Will stopped by to do regular check-ins to see how they were getting along. Aiya's feedback was always positive.

"Aiya, you know he is going to have to meet the family. I know you've never lied to your mom, but I just need you to withhold the whole truth. Most of all I need it to be believable. This is working; paparazzi have been posting pictures of you guys for the last month or so. Someone even snapped a photo of you smacking someone. Caption read 'A Bad Girl For the Bad Boy'. The fans have been eating it up. They are actually playing his music again."

Will barely stopped to take a breath. Once he did, Aiya interrupted him.

"Will, I think it is time for him to meet the parents. I never thought I'd be saying that especially where he is concerned. By the way how is Uncle Joey?"

Will simply threw up his hand, in a haphazard wave. He

shook his head letting her know don't ask. Once Will left, Aiya decided to make the call. No need to procrastinate or drag this out any longer than it had to be. She made a mental note to ask Will how long this was supposed to last, she knew he had a complicated relationship with his father and saw this job as his chance to bond with his father. Joey B left town a few years ago to start recruiting new talent. He was rarely around; which Will didn't mind. That just meant his father wasn't constantly looking over his shoulder while he was trying to build a clientele. Joey B is Frances' older brother. Well half-brother, to be exact. Aiya didn't see too much of Joey these days. He and her mother had a disagreement when their father passed from colon cancer eight years ago. The crazy thing was they disagreed about how and where to bury their father. He left no living will, and neither of them were named power of attorney over his affairs. From that moment on Joey was always in the wind, trying to sign the next big act. He had a few stars under his belt and seemed to be doing well for himself.

The plans were made to leave for home that weekend. As the day drew closer Aiya felt uneasy. She didn't like lying to her parents. In all her years, she never had, well not to this extreme anyway. Aiya tried to remind herself that it was for the greater good and she was helping her family with the medical bills from her granny. She knew her parents were struggling to make ends meet. They were on a fixed income. Both parents retired from government jobs a few years ago, but even their pensions were barely enough to pay their bills with a few scraps to live off. Thankfully their family home was paid for.

Ahmad decided it would be best for him to drive her home. He picked her up in his midnight black Hummer H3T, which he added all the bells and whistles. He had upgraded the tires and rims to 20's, but of all his vehicles this was the most conservative. He didn't want to turn her parents off from the start. His stomach was a bundle of nerves. Never in all his adult life had he met the parents of any woman he was dating. Commitment was a foreign language to him. Any time a woman started acting too clingy or serious he bailed on her. A part of him wanted nothing more than for Aiya to be clingy. So far, he hadn't been able to get a true read on her and where she stood with all of this. A part of him wished the deal wouldn't end.

Ahmad was prompt with picking her up. He put her bag into the backseat, after he opened the door for her to get in. Aiya grinned as she told him,

"Who knew the bad boy was so full of chivalry?"

Ahmad only smiled in reply. He liked her teasing. She was right though; he wasn't typically so gentlemanly with the others in the past. The two decided to leave around 10 am Friday morning. That would allow them some time to stop for breakfast on the way.

"Where would you like to eat Aiya?" he asked looking ahead for breakfast options.

"Just somewhere simple, a Waffle House would be nice or perhaps an IHOP."

Using his navigation system, he located the nearest IHOP. They decided to eat in, Aiya wanted to go over some information that he should know and get some more info on him as well. Once they were seated, the quizzing began.

"What is my favorite color?" She asked.

"That is too easy, blue. Your car is blue, you wear blue a lot."

Aiya shook her head in disagreement."Yes, my car is blue, and it is one of my favorites. It isn't the favorite. My absolute favorite is purple. This isn't working out already. I think I should just tell you the information, that will make it much easier for you. It's not going to be believable if these simple questions trip us up."

"Wait, wait ask me another, I bet I will get it right. If I do, you must kiss me right here, right now but, if I'm wrong, you can name anything you want."

That was a bet she could not resist.

"I will take you up on that one. Are you ready?"

Ahmad nodded shyly, "Yes ma'am."

"Okay, you are asking for it. When is my birthday?"

On the inside Ahmad was jumping up and down, she underestimated him. He knew this one for sure. When Will told him his plan to get him back into the good graces of his fans, he inquired about her age and her upbringing. He wanted to ensure she wasn't just a gold digger. That is after he disagreed for hours. Confident as he wanted to be, he stated,

"Hmm… let me see, I do believe the answer is May 4th for 500.00 Alex. And I will be happy to take my kiss here and now my lady."

Aiya couldn't believe he got it right, but a bet was a bet. She refused to renege. She slowly raised up from her seat, walked around to his side of the table, cupping his face in her hands she gave him a sensual, full of promise, type kiss. She could feel his lips smiling against hers. Aiya swore she heard him sigh on the exhale. Before returning to her own seat, she planted a kiss on his forehead, left eyelid, then the right one, one on the tip of his nose, and a final one to his lips again. He reached his arms up to pull her close.

"Ahem, pardon me, your food is here," the waitress interrupted. Aiya walked back around to her seat, feeling full of herself.

"Remember you made the bet. I only paid my debt."

Ahmad couldn't say anything at that moment, she was right. Her debt was indeed paid in full. Of course, none of this helped the fact, she wanted to feel his lips against hers, since the first kiss. Being who she is, she couldn't help but add a little extra, Aiya wanted him to want her kisses too. This was a dangerous game she was playing. Eventually their deal would be over, and she may end up on the losing side. Making a quick mental note to herself, she needed to keep it professional. Besides they never talked about affection being a part of this deal. They ran through some more questions while eating. Ahmad was still warmed up from the kiss and the teasing banter they exchanged. Thinking to himself, he couldn't let her know that she had gotten to him. After breakfast they got back on the road, conversation was very light. Neither of them really knew what was going on inside the other's head. And no one wanted to show their hand yet.

The second part of the drive seemed like the longest car ride ever to them both. When they arrived at her parents' home, he played the gentleman role exquisitely. Ahmad opened her door and escorted her up to the door. When her father answered, he seemed surprised.

"Baby girl, I didn't know you were bringing someone with you."

Ahmad extended his hand for a shake, while he introduced himself to her father.

"Mr. Jones, it is a pleasure to finally meet you. Your daughter has told me quite a bit about you and the Mrs. My name is Ahmad or AJ for short."

James shook the outstretched hand,

"I would say it is a pleasure to meet you Ahmad, but I knew nothing of this. My daughter is usually pretty forthcoming about relationships or friendships. I do recall seeing an article in one of the papers, something about a bad girl for a bad boy."

He glared over the top of his glasses at Ahmad and then back to his daughter.

"Daddy don't be like that; you know the tabloids will do whatever and say whatever to sell papers. Where is Momma?"

Ushering the couple inside, James called to his wife, Frances, to come see who decided to come home.

"Baby, baby, look who is here."

"My baby girl is home," she hugs and kisses Aiya. "And who is this you have with you?"

"Momma, this is Ahmad, my boyfriend. Before you say

anything Momma, I know I should have told you, but I wanted to make sure it would work first. So far so good."

Ahmad intervenes, "I do realize this must seem sudden and out of the blue. May I take you both to dinner, so we can get better acquainted? That is if you haven't already made plans for dinner."

"We'd like that," Mr. Jones said under his breath.

Aiya, asked Ahmad to get her bag from the car, and told him he could freshen up if he liked. He took her up on that offer, truthfully, he was glad for the escape. When he returned from the truck, she showed him where to put her bag. He noticed her room was full of art. He had to admit she was very talented. Ahmad told her as much when she came up behind him.

"You know, no guy besides my dad has ever been in this room. I'm surprised my dad didn't tell you that he would bring the bag up himself."

"It doesn't seem as if your parents are too fond of either me, or the idea that you have someone in your life."

"They are just protective is all, especially my dad. They have been through a lot and dealing with my granny's declining health hasn't been easy."

To be perfectly honest Ahmad had never dealt with a family member being ill. Once his mom left it was just him and his pops. He clung to his boys, because they were the only other family he had. Since his last stint in rehab, they had lost touch. He was a little hurt that they didn't come to see him, or even answer his calls. Will told him to focus on him and his career. He had begun working on some music while in rehab. Ahmad was eager to get to work but he wanted to make sure people would respond well.

"Ahmad, where did you go? You zoned out on me there."

"I'm sorry love, I was just thinking about family. My pops don't know I'm home either. So why haven't you told your parents about me?"

"I figured the less they knew the better, I don't like lying to them. This is only my sixth time ever doing it and I feel horrible. The other times it was over minor stuff. I skipped school one day and that was about as much of a rebel I ever was."

Ahmad pulled her in for a hug, it was spontaneous, but he had no control over it. When Aiya exhaled he realized he was good.

"Baby girl, how much time do you need before you both are ready to go?" her father bellowed from downstairs.

"Coming Daddy. Be right there."

Ahmad attempted to call his pops but got no answer. Thinking to himself, he would try him again tomorrow. He needed to focus on being the dutiful boyfriend.

Ahmad let Mr. Jones decide where they would eat at. He chose a Japanese one, which was Aiya's favorite.

Ahmad offered to drive everyone, but her father declined. He stated they may go check on his mother before returning home. Aiya protested and said they could all go, but her dad stood his ground, saying that it may be too much for her to take in all at once. Ahmad said they would meet her parents at the restaurant, he wanted to run by his pops' house to see if he wanted to join them for dinner. At that moment his phone blared out. It was Will. Ahmad asked him if he had heard from his pops. Will told him that he was out of town. He and some friends were down in Georgia. Ahmad just shrugged it off, because he knew he had disappointed his father for the last time. He showed it by never coming to visit him, or so much as giving him a call.

The drive to meet her parents was a silent one. Aiya had a lot on her mind. Being at home saddened her. She knew it was only a matter of time before her granny would lose the fight with her illness. Aiya knew that would devastate her father more than anything.

When they arrived at the restaurant, James and Frances were

waiting. The hostess showed them to their seats. As always Ahmad was a perfect gentleman. He pulled out Aiya's chair for her, waited for her to sit, as well as her mom. The men made small talk, while Aiya and her mom chatted about a sale that was going on. Frances inquired as to how long it would be before she opened her gallery.

"Mom you know I'm still saving up for that. Besides, I don't have enough pieces to get it up and going yet. Once I get some more done, I'm going to host a local talent exhibition to get some of the children some exposure."

Grabbing her daughter's hand, "You do know we are so very proud of you, don't you? Your father and I are sorry to be such a burden on you."

Aiya shook her head yes.

"What do you think of Aiya's talent Ahmad?", her father threw in.

"Today is the first day that I have actually seen it up close and personal. Your daughter is very talented. She has been a godsend to me."

The rest of dinner went off without a hitch. Aiya couldn't believe how well her parents were handling the whole thing with Ahmad.

When they arrived home, Aiya was heading up the stairs with Ahmad but, her father calls her back down for a moment. Ahmad continued up the stairs but hung back halfway up to see if he could hear what was going on downstairs. Her mother starts in first.

"Aiya, you know we have never tried to hinder you or your growth with a lot of nagging. But your father and I are concerned. Ahmad seems nice enough today. With you it seems he is head over heels."

"What your mother is trying to say is, we know who he is and what he is. This guy has been in and out of rehab so much, they have a bed reserved for him. What are you doing with him?

You can do so much better. Do you think he has honestly changed?"

Aiya had never felt double-teamed by her parents the whole time she was growing up, until now.

"Daddy, you don't know what you are talking about. Yes, he has made some bad decisions in the past but who hasn't? He has been nothing but a perfect gentleman with me. Just because someone has a past it doesn't have to dictate their future. I like him a lot, perhaps I'm even falling for him. If that is something you can't handle then, we don't have to be here. We will leave."

"Baby girl that is not what I'm saying. Your mom and I just don't want to see you hurt. He is a drugged-out playboy at best."

"You're wrong Daddy. Did he act like that today?"

Frances butted in, "Well no he didn't, but he was putting on a show for us. Baby you said it yourself before, when he was still at the club occasionally. He is an arrogant twit and those are the exact words you used. Although I could be wrong."

"Well Mom, that was before I truly got to know him. And I can say it has been great. Yes, I'm cautious because of who he is. At the end of the day it's my life. And for now, I'm choosing him. No Daddy, not over you and Mom. Just in general. I deserve to be happy for once. I'm always giving to others. It's time I take something for myself."

Everyone became silent. They knew where she was going with her statement without her completing the rest. She was tired. Aiya was the glue keeping the family together in more ways than one.

Ahmad cautiously hurried up to the room. He could hear Aiya coming up the stairs stomping. Which was a big feat for her, as she was a tiny-framed young lady. He could hear every step she took from her 130lb frame. Ahmad had never seen her this mad. He hated to admit but it caused him to get turned on. Ahmad walked over to her and pulled her close for a hug. At that moment she felt safe and sighed a breath of relief. As much as she tried to fight it, the tears began to fall. Ahmad was taken aback that yet again she had defended him. This wasn't something he was familiar with. He had become immune to the stones the tabloids threw at him. Ahmad knew she was emotional right now, so he put it in the back of his mind to be mindful if she expressed her feelings again. Interrupting his thoughts, she lifted her head. Their eyes locked briefly as their lips connected.

FIVE

AHMAD

Ahmad's mind was in a frenzy.

He couldn't believe that she melted into him like that. Oh my God, she felt like heaven. He had wondered if her lips were as soft and smooth as they felt during the kiss at the restaurant. Ahmad tried to pull away, only to be held onto for dear life by Aiya. He couldn't resist her any longer.

Wrapping his arms around her, he pulled her completely into the room. Closing the door hurriedly behind him. He scooped her up and placed her on the bed. Ahmad's eyes never left hers, as if he was waiting for confirmation to continue. He didn't see what he was looking for in her eyes.

"Aiya, do you want me to stop?"

"No," came the faint whisper, as it barely escaped her mouth.

Ahmad began kissing her neck and making a trail down to her breast. He paused there as he clumsily unbuttoned her top and removed it. Ahmad nearly took her arm off as well, but she didn't seem to mind at that moment. Her breast was partially exposed, and he could see that her nipples were standing at attention. This ardent response to his touch, only excited him further.

He could feel himself stiffening up. At that moment Aiya grabbed each side of his face and held his eyes so she could look deep into his soul. Gently she kissed each of his eyelids. He looked down and noticed her bra unfastened from the front. He made quick work of ridding her of that. He teased himself as he slowly began revealing what he thought was the most perfect set of breasts he had ever seen. Aiya laid back onto the bed, sliding herself up so that she was completely on the bed. Ahmad pulled himself away, never losing her gaze, as he pulled his pullover polo up over his head. A smile played across Aiya's face. She had often thought of how he looked naked. This was even better than her mind had imagined.

Unable to resist herself she slid to the end of the bed, to where he stood. Aiya glided her nails across his chest, back and finally his stomach. She reveled in the fact that his body was betraying him. His eyes had closed, he became engrossed in his own world. Ahmad didn't even notice when she started unfastening his pants. It wasn't until he heard the jiggling of his keys and felt a slight breeze that he knew what had occurred. There he stood, with just his Calvin Klein boxers on, and his pants around his ankles. His package was just sitting there, begging to be released from the confines of his boxers. Aiya looked at it and looked at him.

"Are you sure", he asked.

Pulling the corner of her bottom lip into her mouth, she shook her head yes. As much as Ahmad wanted to take her, he didn't want it to be something she would regret. He held back his excitement. Ahmad wanted more than anything for this to mean something to her. But as soon as she looked up at him, with those eyes, he knew he would give her the world.

Aiya sensing his hesitation, pushed him slightly, so she could stand. Without breaking his gaze, she slowly slid her capris down and stepped out of them. She moved around him and walked over to the door to make sure it was locked. Frances had a habit of bursting into her room without knocking. The last thing she wanted her mom to see was his Calvin Klein boxers or her black lacy thong. Aiya was sure her mom would never get over that. *What a time to be thinking about her mother.* Ahmad quickly recaptured her attention, as soon as she was within reach. He grabbed her hand and pulled her toward him.

Aiya placed one hand upon his chest and the other she let linger just close enough to his piece. It twitched against her hand. She knew he was doing it on purpose. Ahmad spun her around so he could get a good look. As if she read his mind, she pulled her panties down exposing her most prized possession. Ahmad stepped back to take her beauty in. Her body was perfect in every way. He picked her up from the waist, so she wrapped her legs around his hips. Carrying her to the side of the bed and he was about to lay her down, but she wouldn't unwrap her legs. Instead she used the heel of her feet to slide his boxers down. Aiya's lips were on his, so he wouldn't intervene in her full-on assault. Her nails were digging into his back. His breathing became labored. Ahmad slid himself inside of her. He felt her tense up. Ahmad was prepared to stop but she whispered in his ear.

"No baby please don't stop. I'm okay, I promise."

She flickered her tongue lightly on this neck. Aiya bit down and that drove him over the edge. Ahmad slid into her again. She was warm and wet. It was as if her treasure was made just for him. Aiya gasped. This sensation was one she wasn't used to feeling. Her body had betrayed her. With each thrust she succumbed more and more.

When Ahmad's legs began to weaken, he laid her on the bed, still inside of her. Their lovemaking only intensified. He kissed her deeply as his thrusts deepened hitting that perfect angle deep inside. When he felt her walls tightening around him, he took her breast into his mouth. Gently he bit down onto her nipple. She released her nectar onto him.

Aiya was cradling his head against her chest. He rolled over onto the bed so as not to crush her. Aiya kissed his forehead. This was the way they drifted off to sleep.

SIX

AIYA

Aiya woke before Ahmad.

God even in his sleep he was handsome.

He looked so peaceful. It was apparent that he was comfortable in his own skin. Aiya had awakened previously and put on a night shirt. She literally had to pry his arm from around her. *If only all of this was real.*

Smiling to herself, she heads downstairs. It was odd that everyone was still sleeping at 8:30. Aiya took this opportunity to make breakfast for the family. She decided to make French toast one of her mom's favorites. Frances would never fix it for herself, she would always say Aiya's tasted like heaven. *If her mom only knew what she had just been a part of last night, she might view her angel status a little differently.* Aiya turned on the tv and was watching the news as she gathered what she needed from the fridge.

Aiya began replaying the events of last night. It was sad to say but that was only her second time being with a guy. All kinds of thoughts ran through her mind. *What if he could tell she was inexperienced? What if he regrets what happened? Will this ruin their agreement? Please God, I need this money to take care of*

Granny's expenses. The more she thought about it, the one thing she did know is that she didn't regret it. Aiya enjoyed it and she could see why she was so into him before. Although he never seemed to have noticed her.

Frances was the first down the stairs.

"Yum! What is that I smell? My baby girl has to be in the kitchen."

Sniffing in the air, "I smell French toast, turkey bacon, scrambled eggs with cheese and Cream of Wheat."

Frances walked into the kitchen and kissed Aiya on the cheek and hugged her from behind. It was days like that, that Aiya missed living at home. However, she didn't miss conversations like the one they had last night.

"I got a call from the hospice center this morning around 7. Nanna is declining more and more each day. She is refusing food again."

They had already inserted a feeding tube to try to keep some fluids in her.

"Last night she had a fall. This is the third one in little over a week. She is lucky to only have a bruised hip this time. I know your dad wants to keep her here for as long as he can. Lord knows she is fighting to be here. I just know that it is a struggle for her to even breathe on most days. The one thing I am sure of is that God is in control."

Aiya hugged her mom tightly. Just as her dad came down the stairs. Aiya kissed her father on the cheek.

"I love you Daddy even if you are stubborn as an old mule."

Before he could object, Aiya told him,

"Just kidding Dad, well sort of... Breakfast is ready for you."

She proceeded to make Ahmad a plate with a bit of every-thing. She still was not sure about what he ate or preferred. One thing she was almost positive about was that he exerted some energy last night and would probably be starving. She smiled to herself as she made her way back upstairs.

As she quietly opened the door to her room, she came face to face with Ahmad.

"I'm sorry."

He knew he startled her. Ahmad had awakened to just an empty bed. This was a first for him. Immediately he felt that he hadn't satisfied her or worse yet, she felt forced because of their arrangement. Ahmad couldn't stomach the thought that he had pushed her or taken advantage of her. He was so enthralled with her coming to his defense. Ahmad couldn't deny it, that single act turned him on. No one had ever really stood up for him before. A part of him felt that he owed her for doing that.

When she wasn't lying beside him, Ahmad got up and took a long shower. His mind was all over the place. By the time she came upstairs with a plate of food in her hand, he was dressed for the day. Aiya was smiling as she entered the room. Ahmad immediately grabbed the tray of food from her grinning.

"Is all of this for me?"

Aiya smiled, "Yes. I wasn't sure what you would want so I brought you some of all of it."

Again, Ahmad was touched.

"You are going to eat some of this, I hope. It all looks very good. Thank you so much for being so great. Not just for this, but with everything. I know it can't be easy. I never wanted to put you and your folks at odds especially over me."

Aiya couldn't believe what he was saying. *After what they had shared, she thought they were connecting on a whole different level. This conversation seems as if they were breaking up or that he felt regret.*

"You didn't put my family and I at odds. Are you talking about the conversation from last night? Okay, of course it wasn't my best conversation but that was my choice. I didn't do it for you. I did it because of you."

"That's just it Aiya, you shouldn't have to be put in that position. I never want you to feel pressured to defend me. Last night was great. I have no regrets, but I feel as if you do. I want to apologize to you, that was never meant to be a part of the deal. You were emotional last night, and I feel as if I took advantage of you and your kindness."

During the whole conversation he had been looking out of her bedroom window not meeting her gaze. He knew he couldn't allow himself to get lost in those eyes.

"I think we just need to stay professional so that things don't get complicated."

Aiya walked over to him, grabbing his chin and turning it slightly so he had to look at her.

"Say it to my face. Say it now."

Ahmad tried to turn his face, but she wasn't letting go.

"Aiya you are an amazing woman. So, let's agree that you and I should remain strictly professional. Things will work much better that way."

"Fine Ahmad, we will be professional. Maybe it is for the best."

Aiya turned away hurriedly and went straight to the bathroom. She was unable to keep the tears from falling. *Why am I crying? It's not like he is mine or I belong to him. It is just an arrangement. Get that through your skull Aiya.* Ahmad knocked on the door.

"Aiya are you okay?"

Instead of replying to him, she turned the shower on. Ahmad took his cue and went and sat down to eat his food.

SEVEN

AHMAD

By the time Aiya finished with her shower, Ahmad was no longer in the room. He was downstairs, chatting with her parents. Frances was keeping him entertained with some of Aiya's antics as a child.

Ahmad was starting to feel that maybe her family was starting to warm up to him after all. He admitted it was a good feeling to be a part of a family again. That was something that he missed out on for far too long. His father showed him love but it was more tough love than anything else. Aiya's family genuinely showed each other that they love and cared for each other, even if they don't agree all the time.

James was flipping through the entertainment section of the newspaper.

"Frances, come look at this."

He was pointing to the paper, when she turned and looked at him, he began flapping it about.

"This sounds like fun. I didn't realize that it was already that time of year."

"James you know it is tradition. I wonder if the kids would like to go also." She said looking back over to Ahmad.

"I'm game if Aiya is. I remember going to this before."

He paused for a moment. Frances was the first to speak up.

"Well then, that is even more reason for us to go. Aiya come downstairs please," Frances yelled.

Aiya yelled back, "Be down in just a second Momma."

Aiya was not ready to face Ahmad yet. Even though they had both agreed to keep it professional and business like, she still was bothered that he seemed to have regretted the love that was made between them. Maybe she was too needy or too aggressive. Whatever it was she intended for it not to happen again. She hated to admit that she did enjoy his friendship more than she thought she would. What Aiya knew for sure was that she was going to play the role she was getting paid for.

Ahmad was thinking about how she was going to act when she came downstairs. To his surprise, she was calm, cool, and collected as she entered the kitchen. He watched as she went to her father and gave him a kiss on the cheek and a hug. She then went to her momma and did the same. Aiya turned to walk towards Ahmad, he stood up from his chair and he walked towards her.

"Hey Babe, your parents were just asking if we wanted to check out the Spring Fling Fair, it's going on today and tomorrow."

He was taken aback when Aiya reached out to hug him. Ahmad was even more stunned when she stood on her tiptoes to kiss him on the cheek. He towered over her, Ahmad was well over 6ft tall, compared to Aiya's 5ft 4inch frame, she was very petite compared to Ahmad. When they made love, she fit into his arms perfectly.

They agreed to let Ahmad drive them to the fair. Aiya felt like her conversation got through to them. At least they were trying to be cordial. When Ahmad pulled up to the fairgrounds, he could immediately smell the turkey legs being smoked. He spotted the funnel cake truck, which was always one of his favorites. One of his fondest memories that he shared with his father was attending the fair. It was a time before the fame and the drugs brought about the destruction of their family. Ahmad had pulled as close as he could because Mrs. Frances had a slight limp in her right leg. So, he was trying to get as close as he could to the entrance so as to not inconvenience her with a long walk. During the car ride he was smiling, cracking jokes. Ahmad felt that they were starting to come around.

Once they had parked, Ahmad walked around to open the door for Aiya, and then Frances. He was trying to get all the brownie points he could today. Ahmad walked Frances around to her husband, and he took her hand from there. They were cute, walking hand in hand. James looked at his wife with such love in his eyes. This type of open affection was something that Ahmad wasn't used to. Even though he tried to hide it, his father would run through women like water. He tried to keep that lifestyle away from Ahmad, but he saw it, and if he didn't see it, he heard about it in the streets. Ahmad would get a taste for this lifestyle himself later during his days in the industry. For that moment he would be happy, but it never lasted long. In retrospect, he knew this was the kind of love that he wanted. He wanted to grow old with someone, maybe have a family, and travel. Although the Jones' were going through some financial struggles due to James' mother's condition, they still enjoyed life to the fullest and didn't let the hard times bring them down. Looking over at Aiya, she deserves this type of love, right? If he thought it would work, he would have loved to be the one standing next to her in fifty years. That is if this was real. Sometimes he felt like it was, she was one hell of an actress. He was even starting to believe.

"Ahmad…Ahmad, where did you just drift off to?"

"Nowhere babe. Just got lost in my own thoughts. The smell of the turkey wings took me back in time. But, hey I am back and ready to have some fun. So where are we headed to first?"

"Umm… obviously we are going to get you a turkey leg.

Perhaps before we leave if you are a good boy, we will get the baby a funnel cake."

Although she was being a wise guy, Ahmad couldn't help but smile. *She did listen to me.* He thought smugly

"Wait, can we go get on the Ferris Wheel first?"

Aiya couldn't resist him when he flashed that million-dollar grin. He had this boyish charm about him and if she didn't keep her head, she would fall head over heels for him. Who was she kidding, she was already heading down that road. Truth of the matter, she didn't regret it. For once she wasn't thinking about her future, and planning ten steps ahead, she was enjoying only her here and now. Her now consisted of spending as much time with Ahmad and just enjoying life.

"Yes, I guess we can. If you promise to stop acting like a five-year-old."

Ahmad simply nodded that he would behave himself.

The two went on several rides, and then they were about to meet up with Aiya's parents to have lunch. Ahmad was surprised to see that James also loved funnel cakes and turkey legs. The two men talked like they were old friends. Even Frances relaxed in Ahmad's presence. He knew without a doubt that they loved their daughter and would do anything to protect her. Shifting his thoughts, he told the Jones' that he would be inviting them to his next show. They smiled but he knew they wouldn't come. Still it felt good to offer it genuinely.

After their food had settled, the two couples decided to give the fair one last go around before they headed back home. Frances didn't want to complain, but Aiya knew that she was getting tired. She was so happy to have her daughter home she was pushing through. Frances had sat too long and her muscles were beginning to get tight. They were so into their conversation they didn't realize almost two hours had passed.

They made their way through the fair and was just about to head out when Ahmad said he wanted a funnel cake to take with him. He turned around to look for the vendor, and he almost ran smack into two ladies. They recognize him but continued their dash for the restroom.

"Babe, I'm going to run over there really quick to grab us two funnel cakes to take back. If you want to go ahead and walk your parents out, I promise to be quick."

"Mom, Dad do you want something?" They shook their heads no. Her mom was rubbing her knee.

"Alright Ahmad, go ahead, just let me get the truck keys. That way Mom can get off her leg."

"Thank you, baby, but I'm fine. We can wait."

Frances said, waving her hand dismissively.

It fell on deaf ears. Ahmad had already given Aiya his keys and was headed to get in line. Before leaving he gave her a chaste kiss on the cheek. Aiya had a puzzled look on her face for a few seconds. She was expecting more. She'd ask him about it later. Ahmad was in line for all of two minutes when he could hear giggling behind him. Discreetly he tries to turn to see what was going on, but when he did, he made eye contact with one of the ladies. Their eyes locked for a few seconds. He quickly turned back around. Ahmad played it as if he was merely looking around at his surroundings. He learned from listening to their conversation, the one who's eyes he locked with, her name was Rachel.

"Hey, aren't you AJ? I was telling my girl Rachel that it was you."

She said while pointing to her friend.

"We are some of your biggest fans by the way."

Ahmad smiled and said he was, and that he was honored to meet them. Turning back around he thought that was the end of the conversation, but no such luck.

Rachel tapped him on his shoulder. "Simone is your absolute biggest fan. She has always wanted to meet you. Can we get a picture of you and each of us?"

Ahmad was used to this type of attention, although it had been awhile, and he didn't miss it. Since he and Aiya were an item, even if it was a fake one, he was perfectly happy.

Rachel snapped a few pictures of Simone and Ahmad. He didn't even notice until it was too late that Simone had gotten close to his face as if she was going to kiss his cheek. Instead she opted to whisper in his ear.

"We are more than willing to show you a good time tonight."

While saying this to him, she grabbed his hand and placed it on her breast, she acted shocked as Rachel was still snapping away. By the time Ahmad had withdrawn his hand, he saw that she had a clear bag with some white powder right between her breasts. He wouldn't have seen it except when he was pulling his hand away, he pulled at her shirt slightly.

"Come on, we know you like to party."

"I have been clean for a while now. You know what, maybe it wasn't a good idea to take these pictures with you ladies."

Ahmad moved from his place between them and started walking away.

"We just wanted to have a good time. We didn't mean any harm. Once you live the party lifestyle, you will always party. A leopard doesn't change his spots."

Ahmad didn't even respond as he walked away. He couldn't wait to get back to Aiya. Truthfully, he had done well with controlling his addiction. He wasn't going back down that road. Initially this was about getting back on top in the music world, but he was enjoying the benefits of clean living. Ahmad loved the idea of remembering who he was spending time with, and for the first time in a long time enjoying it. His mind was clear, and his senses were firing on all cylinders. Ahmad had begun writing a little when he wasn't with Aiya. He was amazed that what he wrote was good. Having your thoughts unclouded was starting to feel amazing to him.

As he was getting into the truck, Aiya looked over concernedly and asked what was wrong. He looked spooked.

"Nothing is wrong, stood in line all that time and they didn't have any funnel cakes. I am so sorry it took so long," he apologized to James and Frances.

He never meant to keep them waiting for so long. Aiya could tell something was wrong, but she didn't want to ruin their good day. She reached over and grabbed his hand and held it, as he put the truck into gear and began to drive off. In his side mirror he could see the girls getting in their car. *I hope this doesn't come back to haunt me in some way.*

The ride back to Aiya's parents' home was filled with pleasant conversation. They each seemed to take turns recounting the best parts of the day. Ahmad was at ease, because the good vibes he had been receiving all day from James and Frances seemed to continue.

Before they got home, they decided it would probably be best to grab some food and take it home. No one much felt like cooking supper that night after the busy day they've all had. Aiya was surprised when Frances said she wanted some Peruvian-Style Roast Chicken with Tangy Green Sauce. There was a place not too far from home that she loved to eat at. Don Felix had the best roast chicken and sometimes she would get it with spicy cilantro sauce. They would pair it with a delicious avocado tomato cucumber salad that was to die for. Frances' eyes lit up as she spoke about it. Ahmad would not have lived it down if he hadn't accommodated her request, after all they were such gracious hosts.

EIGHT

AIYA

Aiya was consumed by her own thoughts. She was happy that her parents seemed to accept the relationship that she was in with Ahmad. She smiled to herself, as she used her Ice Cube voice.

Today was a good day.

Just then Ahmad entered the room, half knocking as he walked in.

"Ahmad, what was wrong earlier, when you came back to the truck? I know it was something so don't tell me it wasn't."

Walking closer to Aiya, Ahmad reached for her hand.

"I have just been doing some thinking. It just kind of hit me earlier, that thanks to you, I have really been doing this sober and clean thing right. I don't miss the attention, none of it. The partying or getting high. My name is finally not being splashed in the headlines every other day. I owe a lot of this to you."

Aiya was taken aback, he spoke as if he meant it, and he didn't break eye contact not once. She stepped into his arms. This is where she felt she belonged. She hated to think that this would all be coming to an end soon. Aiya was determined to ride it out for as long as they could. He wasn't this self-centered egotistical jerk she thought he was. Her heart was starting to allow him in more and more as the days passed. She wondered what he was thinking about all this. At that moment Ahmad exhaled but his grip around her waist tightened. She had almost forgot she was in his arms. Aiya lifted her head and placed a kiss on his lips. He in return kissed her forehead and then her left eyelid and finally her right.

Ahmad brought his hands to each side of her face.

"Babe, I want you so much. I know we made a deal to keep it professional. If you want me to stop I will. Just say the word."

Before Aiya could respond, Ahmad turned her around so her back was resting against his chest. She knew he wanted to know she had stirred him. With a quick movement she raised her arms to wrap them around his neck. He slid his fingertips down her sides. She squirmed a little, and he was enjoying the feel of her against him. Ahmad slid his hands underneath her shirt and up her sides. This was different that just a few seconds ago.

It was as if he knew exactly where to touch her, for her world to catch fire. Aiya stepped away from him, reaching for his hand and led him to the bathroom. Ahmad sat on the side of the tub and pulled her down onto his knee. Aiya leaned over to run some water. Ahmad wouldn't relax his grip.

"Ahmad, I'm not going far, I promise."

"Since you promised. I'm keeping my eye on you."

"Good, keep watching. Let me know what you think?"

She purposely dragged out the word think. By the time she had finished the word, her shirt was raised to show the bottom of her breast. Ahmad could not contain his excitement and a growl escaped his lips. She instinctively bit down on the corner of her lip.

She continued her striptease; she noticed he was watching the water levels in the tub. He had plopped a jasmine and a lavender bath bomb in, and the fragrance was swirling around them, softly perfuming the air.

After her shirt, she stepped out of her bottoms, and pulled her thong down at the same time. Ahmad was watching her intently, getting even more turned on as each moment passed tantalizingly slow. He stood up, still watching her, leaned over and turned off the faucet.

His movements were deliberate. She had teased him, and he was going to make sure she suffered a little as well.

Ahmad reached down and unbuckled his belt. He pulled his pants down to the top of his hips. He had a smirk on his face as he flashed his Calvin Klein's, Aiya couldn't deny this was one sexy man. She walked over and started tugging on his pants. His manhood was eagerly awaiting. Aiya took him in her hand and gently stroked up and down. Ahmad was out of his clothes; he couldn't withstand this woman even if he wanted to. He knew he was trying to make her pay, but it would only push him further and further to the edge of his sanity. The crazy part is that she could have been standing there doing absolutely nothing, and he would still be unbalanced. Her effect on him was unmatched.

He sat down in the tub and pulled her to a sitting position where she was straddling him. They began kissing each other. A long slow passionate caress, one of those ones where it felt as if your souls connected on an intrinsic level. At that moment their eyes connected. There wasn't anything he wouldn't do for her, and he feared she might know it.

They took turns washing each other's bodies with gentle, teasing touches. Just when they thought they could take no more, Ahmad slid himself into her. She welcomed him. Aiya dug her nails into his back as he filled her. Their movements were in perfect sync. So much so that when they hit their climax it left them both satiated and spent. They used the last of their strength to wash off, rinse themselves, and climb into bed. Ahmad slept with his arms around her the entire night. He wanted to have a heart to heart discussion tomorrow with her. The song from Toni Tony Tone *Feels Good*, stayed on his mind until he dozed off.

NINE

AHMAD

Ahmad rolled over smiling as he recalled the events of the previous night.

There was just one problem, he was alone in bed. As his eyes began to focus, he noticed a note on the pillow where Aiya had slept. He noticed her handwriting immediately. She had left a note saying that they had to hurry and get to her grandmother, that the hospice center had called, and she wasn't doing well. Aiya said she would see him soon, although she wasn't sure exactly when. She assured him she would let him know what was going on as soon as she could.

Ahmad got up and took his shower. He wasn't exactly comfortable being in their home alone. To be honest, he hadn't stayed over at too many women's homes. Then his mind went to Aiya. He hoped things were okay, but he was also being realistic, he knew the circumstances. He said a quick prayer for the family.

Just then his phone rang. He finished his prayer and returned Will's call.

Ahmad spoke into the phone, "What's up bro? I was in the middle of a prayer for your cousin's grandmother."

Will didn't waste any time; he was yelling into the phone. Ahmad got a few words in but then stopped dead in his tracks.

"Ahmad what is wrong with you? Why do you think we are doing this whole damage control plan for? I even involved my family to help fix your tarnished reputation."

"Bro, what are you talking about? Damage control? I've been with your cousin since the beginning. What's going on?"

"Ahmad, why are you on the freaking news? Tell me why is your face plastered everywhere? And I do mean everywhere. You are the talk of the town, but not just the town. You are back to where you began. Tell me how? Tell me why in heaven's name did you screw up everything we been working towards?"

"I didn't do anything. Man, I swear to you. What are they saying?"

"When did you interact with two women? Better yet, why did you interact with them? These women are saying you are using again. They gave a play by play account of what happened. They said you approached them; they have pictures. The worst part is, they say you were trying to party with them. They were so good with the story they even had a picture of a bag of cocaine. They weren't charged with possession because they were protected as confidential informants. The pictures they used of course had them blurred out. Guess who looks like the same ole druggie troublemaker? Yeah, you guessed correctly. Ding, Ding, Ding…. you have won the grand prize."

Ahmad couldn't believe it. He was hoping that the whole thing was just a simple misunderstanding. He couldn't believe this was happening. Things were going so well.

"Will, you have to believe me. That isn't what happened at all. Aiya and her parents were at the fair. We were all together. The only time we weren't together was when I went to try to get some funnel cakes right before we left. I gave Aiya my keys and headed over to the vendor and stood in line. While there I was approached by these two ladies and things quickly got out of hand. The screwed-up thing is I didn't even get any of the cakes."

"You aren't getting it. You are screwed. I believe you, but I don't think anyone else will. I'm going to have to try and figure this out. Stay put, don't do anything else. I'm not even sure if Aiya has seen this stuff, much less her parents. So please chill. Promise me that you are going to chill out."

"Okay Will, please help me fix it. I have so much to tell you bro, but now isn't the time."

Suddenly the sound of the front door slamming shut echoed throughout the house.

James was yelling at the top of his lungs. "Ahmad or AJ whatever you want to be called. We have tolerated you and our daughter's relationship because she is our daughter. She believed in you, so for her sake so did we. How could you do this to your-self? To her?"

Ahmad hustled down the stairs and tried to explain what happened.

"It wasn't like that at all. I have been clean and sober since before I started dating your daughter. She is the best thing that has ever happened to me."

Before he could finish explaining what happened, James told him to pack his things and get out. He was no longer welcome in their home or anywhere near their daughter. This whole time Frances was just watching from a distance with her cell phone clutched firmly in her hand, she heard that Ahmad used to get rowdy. She wasn't sure just what to expect, but she wanted to be prepared.

Surprisingly he didn't act out with her husband. Frances thought maybe it was a mistake making him leave, but she knew better than to go against James. It didn't help that James' mother had passed that morning, so emotions were running rather high. James and Frances had seen the interview with the girl on the local news while they were at the hospice center. When his mother took her last breath, it was at that moment the tv caught his attention. He went ballistic when he noticed the tv had a picture of Ahmad and the interview that followed.

James just kept yelling. Ahmad couldn't get his stuff together fast enough.

"Sir, if you would just let me explain."

James was having none of it.

"Frances let's go while he gets all of his things. I don't want him to leave any piece of him behind. This is just horrible, Momma's gone and now this wise cracker. Don't think for a moment I'm not keeping my eye on you. Don't take anything that isn't yours."

After about twenty minutes of gathering his belongings and tense silence, Ahmad walked downstairs, looked back at James and Frances, and walked out the door.

This wasn't supposed to happen. He was happy yesterday. Things were going so well. I guess it's true, it only takes a moment for life to go sour.

TEN

AIYA

Aiya was completely devastated after she lost two important people in her life within the same day. When Aiya returned home from getting her grandma's things together, she saw no evidence of Ahmad. Over the last week, things had been hectic. James and Frances kept on and on about the situation with Ahmad. Telling Aiya he was no good for her. Aiya had seen the tabloids and even the media coverage. She didn't want to believe it. He left without saying a word. She had been too focused on making the final arrangements for her granny. James was having a rough time dealing with her loss even though they knew it was coming. James handled his grief by calling Ahmad a good for nothing low-life junkie.

"He wasn't good enough for you. He was a trickster and he fooled us all. Imagine trying to score drugs while we were at the fair."

"Daddy, I love you, but I don't need to hear that right now. Do you want me to say you were right? I won't say that. You didn't know him like I did."

After a week or so, James finally admitted to Aiya that he

was the one who kicked Ahmad out. The family had been going about their business, being pleasant to each other, but there was something missing.

Aiya decided when she saw Will at the memorial service for her grandmother that she wanted to talk to him about getting in touch with Ahmad. Will didn't bring his name up because James was adamant, he didn't want to hear that name in his presence ever again.

A few more days passed, and things had finally calmed down, Aiya decided to reach out to Will, when her father wasn't at home.

"Will, hey whats going on?"

"Not too much Aiya. How about you?"

"What is going on with your boy? Did he do it?"

"Aiya, I honestly don't know. I had my investigator try to locate the two women. They were sticking to their story. My gut feeling is they are just some fame chasers looking for their 15 minutes of fame. Ahmad swears that he didn't do what they said. He even said you all were together. That was enough for me, I still read him the riot act. My job is to get his stuff straightened back out. That has been hard to do because he went off the grid for the last few weeks. I've been to the house, but he won't even answer the door."

"How do you know if he is okay?"

"I truly don't know. I hope he is though. I guess he will come around when he is ready."

"Will, are you serious? What if he went back to truly using?"

"He wouldn't do that," Will didn't sound too convinced about it. "If you want his address, I will give it to you, and you can check on him if you like. Maybe he will respond to you."

"Thanks, Will, I will let you know what I find."

Aiya was just leaving the house as her parents were returning.

"Where are you going baby?"

"I'll be back in a while. I'm going to go see Ahmad. I don't want to hear nothing from you. You guys ran him off. You will be to blame if he does relapse."

Aiya grabbed her keys and headed out the door without looking back.

She was trying to rehearse what she would say when she got there. What if he didn't answer the door or worse yet, he had indeed relapsed? She didn't want her mind to go there either.

Aiya made it to Ahmad's address in record time. He was outside cutting grass. She had never seen him doing anything so normal. Ahmad had a straw hat on his head, and his shirt was off. He looked as good as she remembered. She was watching him; he didn't look like he had relapsed. This made her smile. She parked the car and jumped out before it stopped rolling.

Ahmad couldn't believe she was there. He turned the mower off and walked over to her.

"Hey…."

"What are you doing here?"

"I was worried about you. My dad told me some of what happened. I would have come sooner but I was trying to work things out with my granny's affairs. You know she passed right? The very same day you left. I was lost for a few days, but I had to keep it together for my family. I thought you may have begun using again or drinking again. I'm happy that you aren't though. That proves you have changed. My parents apologize for their behavior. They know it was uncalled for. They should have at least heard you out."

"Babe, I'm sorry, I'm not sure if I have that right. I have missed you so much. I should have told you that night when you asked what was wrong. Aiya, I was hoping that it wouldn't come back to bite me. They were flirting with me and trying to get me to party with them. I turned them down. For the first time in my life, I was truly happy. I was with you.

Your family was coming around. Drugs were the last thing on my mind."

Aiya stepped closer to him, he opened his arms. She fell into them. Finally, she was home again.

"Aiya I know this was just supposed to be fake, but my feelings for you are not. You have become an integral part of my world. A world I don't want to be in without you."

"Ahmad, I should have told you this before, but I love you. I don't know when it happened, but I do. We can fix this, fix us, your career."

For the first time in a long time, Ahmad didn't have a full plan on where he wanted to go next. He did know he wanted to be involved in the music industry. And he knew he didn't want to perform on the regular, he didn't want to take the chance of being away from her and being tempted by all the trappings of fame. He felt he could make a go at finding other talent and helping them reach their dreams. He had become pretty good with writing songs as of late. Perhaps he could get more into the production side. There were endless possibilities.

"Ahmad just think, you can finish school and get your degree in business. You were so close."

Ahmad was touched by the fact that Aiya wanted him to be truly happy doing what he loves. It wasn't ever about the persona with her, she wanted to be with him for him. She wanted Ahmad and not AJ, the bad boy of R&B. For the first time he felt peace settle into his soul. It was like all the pieces just fell into place.

"Aiya, as long as I get to wake up with you, that is all I care about. Are you okay with that? Lord knows I hope you are."

Aiya kissed him full on the lips. This was the beginning of their life together. Ahmad knew he would do anything for her love.

Thank You for Reading....

Don't forget to sign up for
Mind Flow Publishing & Production LLC's Newsletter @
www.mindflowpublishingproduction.com

Email us for autographed or additional paperback copies @
mindflowpubpro@gmail.com

Although I'm still considered new to the publishing world, I have hit the ground running full speed ahead.

In my first year, I was signed to Mind Flow Publishing & Production LLC, and I have published a total of 6 books.

I have earned Amazon's Best Sellers Top 100 orange banner. My works are spread across several genres such as; poetry, inspirational, and Christian fiction. I will be trying my hand at cozy mysteries, romance, and sci-fi. My love for writing started when I was about 12, writing poetry and writing speeches for various oratorical contests. Inspiration for my craft is pulled from my own life experiences, as well as others. I have been featured on several podcasts, as well as Up and Coming Authors Newsletters.

When I'm not writing, I love to design shadowboxes, and create personalized greeting cards. I have released my 3rd poetry book (Spoken from the Heart) in August 2019. I will be releasing a minimum of 2 novellas (For Her Love will be one of them) before the end of 2019.

Current books available are The Mary B Chronicles 1 & 2, Mental Interlude, and Journey to Living, Simple Complexity, and Dreams Do Come True.

All of which are available on Amazon, and www.mindflowpublishingproduction.com.

ALSO BY DAKIARA

<u>Titles Also Available</u>

Mental Interlude – Poetry

The Mary B Chronicles – Fiction

Journey to Living (kindle Kindle only) – Inspirational

Simple Complexity -- Poetry

Spoken From The Heart – Poetry

Dreams Do Come True – Fiction

Available Through

Amazon

Barnes & Noble

Kindle

<u>Coming Soon</u>

For Her LoveThe Mary B Chronicles Book III – Fiction

To Be Chosen Simple Complexity - Poetry

Dreams Do Come True – Paranormal Romance

The Hitchhiker Journey to Living 2 – Inspirational Fiction

A Prince For Me – Romantic Comedy

Forbidden – Romantic Suspense – Fiction

Upcoming Titles Will Be Available Through

Amazon

Barnes & Noble

Kindle

iBooks

Kobo